KT-563-168

# Thorfinn
## and the
# Disgusting Feast

written by David MacPhail

illustrated by Richard Morgan

THORFINN'S VILLAGE

THORFINN'S JOURNEY

# CHAPTER 1

The Viking village of Indgar was nestled beside a
beautiful fjord. Longships floated tied up in the
glassy water, and chimney smoke drifted gently into
the cold, still air. It was a peaceful place, except for
the Vikings themselves, who spent their days either:

a) practising their fighting skills,

b) boasting about how good they were
   at fighting, or

c) just fighting.

It was nearing lunchtime when the smell of barbecued food wafted across the village.

Everyone stopped what they were doing, even those in the middle of a fight. If there was one thing the Vikings loved more than fighting, it was food.

"Oooooh, who's having a barbecue?"

They followed their noses to the marketplace, where a small boy with freckles was standing behind a sizzling charcoal brazier, armed with a wooden spatula. It was Thorfinn the Very-Very-Nice-Indeed, son of the chief.

He had an unusual name for a Viking. Being called Thorfinn the Very-Very-Nasty-Indeed would have been perfectly normal, but Thorfinn wasn't a normal Viking. For a start, most Vikings used pigeons for target practice, but the small, speckled pigeon on Thorfinn's shoulder was his best friend, Percy.

And, most importantly, this boy was NICE. And POLITE. Such things were *very unusual* for a Viking.

"Come along, there's plenty for everyone!" Thorfinn declared as he flipped what looked like a delicious meat pattie between two halves of a bun. "I call it a *burger.*"

He ushered the Vikings into a line. Vikings weren't known to queue, so it really was a sight to behold.

One by one they accepted a burger from Thorfinn.

"Mmmmm!" said one of the Vikings as he wolfed it down. "What kind of meat is in it?"

"I beg your pardon, my dear friend?" replied Thorfinn.

"Venison? Beef? Elk?" the man asked.

Thorfinn shook his head. "It contains no meat at all, I assure you."

Each and every one of the Vikings stopped mid-bite, their eyes wide.

"WHHATTT?"

"They're vegetarian burgers," said Thorfinn. "They're made from vegetables."

# "POO-AAAAAHHH!"

The whole line of Vikings spat out their food.

"That's disgusting, Thorfinn!" cried slimy-haired, warty-faced Gertrude the Grotty. "You shouldn't be cooking that horrible stuff!" She sold specialities like venison-and-earwig pie at her marketplace stall. A sign hanging above it read:

## I ONLY USES FREE-RANGE EARWIGS

At which point the village chief, Harald the Skull-Splitter, appeared on the scene. He was Thorfinn's father, and one of the roughest, toughest and meanest Vikings ever to have lived.

"What's going on here?" demanded Harald.

With him was Erik the Ear-Masher, his second in command. He was almost as grizzly and fierce as Harald, with a face like a bruised cabbage, and only one eye.

"Yes, what's all this noise about?" added Erik.

Erik's son, Olaf, stepped forward. He also had a face like a cabbage, one that had gone off, then been squashed under the wheels of a cart. "It's Thorfinn, Dad. He's trying to poison us!"

"With vegetables!" said one of the other men.

Harald turned and glared angrily at Thorfinn. "What? Is this true?"

Thorfinn smiled, a broad well-meaning smile that would melt anyone's heart – but serving vegetables was a serious accusation.

"Yes, it's true, Father," he beamed. "You know, statistics show that vegetables are very good for you, and our diet is quite meat-heavy."

Erik the Ear-Masher erupted, "Our diet IS meat, you idiot!"

"Yes," added Olaf. "We HATE vegetables."

"DEATH TO ALL VEGETABLES!" cried someone at the back.

The other Vikings roared in agreement, grabbed their axes and hacked the ground to bits all around them. "RAAR! Take that, ground! See, that's how much we HATE vegetables."

Harald turned his ferocious gaze to a tiny girl standing on the sidelines. She wore an oversized helmet and leaned on a massive axe that was almost bigger than she was. It was Thorfinn's friend Velda.

"YOU!" Harald yelled. "You're supposed to be keeping him out of trouble."

Velda shrugged. "I DID tell him. He doesn't listen."

Harald sighed, took his son by the shoulder and led him aside. "Look, boy. You're the cleverest of us all. You've saved this village many times. But you need to be more like your fellow Vikings."

The wise man of the village, Oswald, appeared at his friend Thorfinn's side. He was very old, he had a long white beard and he spoke in an incredibly loud and whiny voice. In fact, he sounded like a donkey having a nightmare.

"If I may say so, Chief, perhaps it is you who doesn't see."

"What do you mean?" asked Harald, his eye twitching at the old man. Harald's eye always twitched when he was angry.

"Thorfinn's a boy of many talents and abilities that the other Vikings don't possess. Perhaps you just need to find the right use for his talents."

"Hmmm..." Harald stroked his chin, but he barely had a chance to consider the old man's suggestion when suddenly the ground started shaking and a noise like thunder filled the air. For a split second Harald looked worried that Thor himself might be about to drop in for a visit.

# CHAPTER 2

The villagers had to dive out of the way as a team of horses leading a huge four-wheeled wagon charged into Indgar. There was a gaggle of people aboard, all laughing and cheering.

Harald coughed and spluttered as he wafted the dust away to reveal the figure of a large man on one of the horses. His old enemy, Magnus the Bone-Breaker, chief of the neighbouring village, was staring down at him.

"What's the meaning of this, Bone-Breaker?"

cried Harald. "You have no right to drive through my village at that speed."

"Oh no? I'd like to see you stop me! I'm selling four-wheel-drive chariot tours of the wild to rich Vikings from down south. Only your stupid village is ruining the view. Now shift!"

He yanked his horse's reins, barging through the angry crowd. Then he stopped and turned, the grin on his face even more smug than before.

"I don't suppose you've heard, but the King himself is coming to tour the fjord."

The crowd gasped.

"The King?" asked Harald. "He's coming here?"

"Yes, in three weeks. He'll be staying at all the villages – in fact he'll be in yours the night after mine. My village will be a tough act to follow." He grinned. "I've got my own chef. Who have you got?" He laughed, a great booming guffaw that echoed around the marketplace. Then he clicked his heels and galloped off.

Everyone was stunned.

It was Thorfinn who spoke first. "This is wonderful news! The King himself. It will be so much fun."

But the rest of them weren't so sure. They gathered round their chief, while Harald stroked his bushy blond beard.

"Hmm. No, this is not good news," said Harald.

"Oh?" said Thorfinn, puzzled. "But there'll be music, dancing, a feast. Perhaps I'm missing something, Father?"

"Magnus is right. If we don't please him we'll be in trouble."

"The King has been known to burn villages to the ground when he gets angry," said Erik. "The Queen is kinder. She's the only one he'll listen to."

Oswald, too, was stroking his beard,

deep in thought. "Then it is the Queen we should seek to please. Her Majesty is said to enjoy exotic delicacies, especially seafood..."

"Yuck! Fish!" cried Olaf.

"That's DISGUSTING!" cried Gertrude the Grotty as she reached down to scoop some ants into her bag.

"Yes, DEATH TO ALL FISH," jeered the crowd.

"We all agree, fish is the most rubbish type of meat," said Erik. "Almost as bad as vegetables. We can't cook fish for the King!"

Harald paced around, shaking his head. "Magnus will try anything to impress. If the King is coming straight from his village, we'll need to get everything right."

Erik groaned. "Then we're stuffed."

Harald went off to throw axes at trees. He did this any time he needed to think. Whenever Harald went for a think EVERYONE rushed indoors. His aim was terrible.

After he finished, he gathered the villagers back into the marketplace. He called Thorfinn and Velda to the front. "I thought about Oswald saying we should use your talents, Thorfinn. I'm putting you in charge of the King's feast."

Thorfinn jumped up and down with excitement.

"That's SOOOOOO great, Father! I'm SOOOOO happy! Thank you."

"Don't thank me yet, son. The King has been known to catapult chefs into the sea."

"You can't put that idiot in charge! He tried to feed us vegetables earlier!" said Erik.

"If anyone can think up an exotic feast fit for the Queen, it's Thorfinn," said Oswald.

"As a matter of fact," Thorfinn said, "I've already had loads of ideas. Oswald is quite correct, if you please the Queen then you'll please the King. So might I suggest we take a boat and go fishing?"

"You really want to cook FISH for the KING? We're doomed!" cried Erik. "And how are you even going to catch them?"

"The Vikings of Indgar have no idea how to catch or cook fish," added Oswald.

"Well then," said Thorfinn. "It might be a good idea to visit Uncle Rolf. He works for the Earl of Orkney in his kitchens. He knows everything about seafood."

"Uncle Rolf, eh? He's the only one in the family who is remotely like you – nice." Harald brightened. "But that is a good idea. Very well, you'll need a ship and a crew."

Thorfinn's face lit up. "My own crew? Really?" He turned to Velda and began jumping up and down again. "I'll be a sea captain!"

"And I'll be your second mate, yelling orders!" cried Velda, who was also jumping up and down. "*Move it, you pig-dogs! Hoist the sail, you swine! Man the oars, you rollicking oafs!* Ha ha, brilliant!"

Erik sighed. "You're really going to give Thorfinn his own ship? And a crew? You're mad!"

Harald ignored his second in command. "Go to Orkney first, learn from Uncle Rolf, and then go fishing." He stood up. "You leave on the next tide, which is tomorrow, one hour after dawn."

Velda began waving her arms around in circles, singing, "*I'm going to sea-ea! I'm going to sea-ea!*"

"Remember," said Harald. "The future of the village is at stake. We're relying on you, Thorfinn. Don't let us down. You have three weeks."

# CHAPTER 3

That night Thorfinn could hardly sleep. He was so excited about going on a voyage with his own crew.

Dawn broke, bright and crisp and beautiful.
He packed up his things and picked some fruit and vegetables from his little garden.

Velda arrived soon after, bouncing over the hill, whistling and carrying her massive axe. "Are you ready, Thorfinn? This is going to be brill."

"I certainly am, dear pal."

Percy flapped onto his shoulder and they set off.

They stopped by Oswald's cottage first, which

was set high on the hillside next to a waterfall.

"We've come to say goodbye, old chum!" Thorfinn called through the window.

"What do you mean, you've come to say goodbye?" said the wise man, sounding like a seal with a bad headache. "I'm coming with you!"

"Are you really, old friend?" said Thorfinn.

"Of course. I'm not hanging about here while you two go off having adventures. Plus, the word on the fjord is that Erik the Ear-Masher has picked the worst crew ever for you, so you'll need back-up. Now come in and sit down while I fetch breakfast."

Thorfinn took a seat at the table. He watched Percy peck up berries, and Velda practise kicking and punching – something she called 'kick-boxing'.

"We're going to catch the best fish EVER," she said. "And if anyone tells us fish is rubbish, I'll knock their block off!" She punched the air.

"Then we're going to make the best feast EVER. And if anyone tries to burn down our village, no matter who they are, they'll have to answer to ME!"

She swung her leg in the air.

She kicked the door – just as Oswald hobbled through carrying a tray!

**CRASH**

Velda froze, her hands clasped to her mouth.

The door wobbled open again, to reveal Oswald
lying on the floor splattered in porridge and jam. The
old man simply shrugged, then spooned some up
with his finger and slurped. "Mmmm... good jam!"

# CHAPTER 4

An hour later the three friends arrived at the pier, where their longship was waiting. The green dragon head on the prow glinted in the sunlight.

The whole village had turned out to see them off. Harald and Erik were waiting at the water's edge.

"Come aboard and meet your crew," said Erik smugly as he led Thorfinn up the gangplank.

It looked like the rumours about the rubbish crew were true. First was Grimm the Grim, the ship's helmsman – in charge of steering the boat. Everything about him was sad. Even his beard seemed droopy.

Thorfinn raised his helmet. "How pleased I am to meet you, Mr Grimm."

"Really?" the helmsman replied in a limp voice. "I'm not very interesting."

"I'm sure you're *very* interesting. Deep down," said Thorfinn hopefully.

"Hmm. It must be very deep down, because I haven't found it yet." Grimm trudged off, his shoulders slouched.

"He's a-laugh-a-minute," said Velda.

Next they greeted the chief warrior on board, Harek the Toe-Stamper. He had a large black beard and a wild look in his eyes, perhaps because they were pointing in opposite directions.

"*Toe-Stamper* – that's a tough-sounding name for a chief warrior," said Thorfinn.

"Yes," said Erik. "Except it's his own toes he stamps on, clumsy oaf."

"I am NOT clumsy," Harek objected and stamped his foot. A loose plank pronged up, which tripped one of the porters, who dropped the barrel he was carrying, which rolled down the boat and smashed into a giant pyramid of barrels, which collapsed, bouncing the barrels into the water one by one.

Harek coughed and looked sheepishly down at the deck.

Then there was Grut the Goat-Gobbler, perhaps the

greediest man in all of Norway. He was quite short for

a man with such a huge appetite.

"He was our only volunteer for this mission," said Erik.

"I heard it was food-related," grunted Grut.

"Is it really true that you once ate an entire goat

in one go?" asked Velda.

"Oh yes," he replied. "Goat is my favourite, apart

from elk, and bear, and beaver, and swan..."

"OK, we get the picture," said Erik. "And talking of food, here's your cook."

It was Gertrude the Grotty, who ran the stall in the marketplace. A squadron of flies were orbiting her head.

"Oh great," said Velda. "So what's for dinner tonight? Ant stew?"

"You haves a choice of menus," Gertrude croaked. "There's wild boar and spider sausages or there's sheep and nits pie." She reached up and plucked something from her scalp then rubbed her fingers together. "The nits gives it a lovely grainy texture. Mmmm."

The crew already looked

seasick, and they hadn't even set sail yet.

"That sounds, er, delightful," said Thorfinn cheerfully. "Though I've brought my own food from the garden."

"I'm eating what Thorfinn's eating!" Velda cut in. "Even if it's vegetables."

"I'm on a diet," said Oswald, who was never on a diet.

Finally, there was Torsten the Ship-Sinker, a tall man with a golden beard. "Now that sounds like a good name for a warrior," said Thorfinn.

"It would be," laughed Erik. "But he's your navigator. He has no sense of direction whatsoever. He's sunk more ships than the kraken that guards the Gates of Valhalla."

"That's not fair!" said Torsten. "You know I get

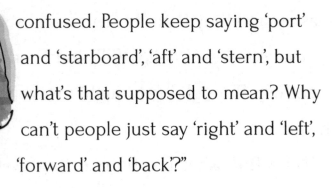

confused. People keep saying 'port' and 'starboard', 'aft' and 'stern', but what's that supposed to mean? Why can't people just say 'right' and 'left', 'forward' and 'back'?"

"Yup," said Velda to Oswald. "You were right. The WORST crew in the world." Also on board was Olaf, Erik's son, sulking at the back. "Oh great," he said. "All the losers of the village on one boat. I would have been hoping you'd sink, but unfortunately I'm coming with you." He cast a sullen glance at his father.

"You're to keep an eye on this lot, Olaf," said Erik. "It'll be good experience for you."

Olaf huffed. "Good experience of getting

shipwrecked, more like."

Harald cast his twitchy eye once more over the ragtag bunch Erik had chosen for Thorfinn's first solo voyage. He glared at Erik, who struggled to hide his smug grin as he stepped down from the boat. But there was no time to lose if they were to get back in time for the feast.

"I trust my son to lead you well," said Harald, gulping. "Now get going." He leapt off the longship. "And don't forget, Thorfinn, we're relying on you."

"I won't let you down, Father," Thorfinn replied.

The gangplank was whisked away, at which point all eyes on board turned to Thorfinn.

"You're the captain. They're waiting for your command," whispered Oswald.

Thorfinn beamed. Then he turned to Velda. "Why, after you, dear friend."

Velda let out a yell that would send shivers up the spine of a banshee. "What are you waiting for? CAST OFF, you miserable weasels! MAN THE OARS, you useless cretins!"

Thorfinn stood at the prow under the green dragon head, with Percy perched on his shoulder. He looked out at the fjords leading to the open sea. "Set sail for the Orkney Islands!"

# CHAPTER 5

Despite Torsten the Ship-Sinker nearly sailing them into the Arctic Ocean, and Grut the Goat-Gobbler eating all the supplies – including Thorfinn's vegetables – they somehow made it to their destination, though it took two days longer than it should have.

"Look, it's the Orkneys!" cried Velda, who was acting as lookout.

They docked at the Earl's castle, which was perched on a rock overlooking a wide bay. The Earl of Orkney was a great Viking prince, whose

43

lands stretched a great distance south onto the mainland of Scotland.

"Why don't we all go ashore and see if Uncle Rolf's in?" suggested Thorfinn. "It'll be a nice group outing for us."

Percy flapped onto Thorfinn's shoulder, and the whole crew marched up to the gates of the castle behind him.

Thorfinn saluted the guard at the gate. "Good morning, my dear sir."

The guard stared, as though Thorfinn had just stepped off a spaceship.

"My name is Thorfinn the Very-Very-Nice-Indeed,

and I'm here to see my Uncle Rolf, who works in your kitchens."

The guard cast his eye over the pigeon on Thorfinn's shoulder and the sorry band of misfits behind him. "Wait here."

It wasn't long before Uncle Rolf – a large man with rosy cheeks and a long twirly moustache – appeared. He was dressed in white and wore a chef's hat. He picked Thorfinn up and gave him a huge bear hug.

"Thorfinn! My nephew's come to visit! What a lovely surprise. Come in!"

He led them through the castle's vast and cavernous kitchens, from one room to another. It was a hot, bustling place, full of shouting and foodie aromas. An army of cooks was chopping, frying, baking, and stirring cauldrons with huge ladles.

Grut was drooling. "Ohhh, that looks nice. That does too. So does that. Mmmmm. Do you mind if I have a taste?" He stopped at every bubbling pot and lagged behind.

Torsten got lost, of course, wandering off in the wrong direction as they turned a corner.

Gertrude was chatting to the kitchen staff. She snatched one of the flies circling her head and offered it to a chef. "Do you wants one of mine for your stew?" The man shook his head in disgust. She shrieked, "No flies? How in the name of Thor do you add any taste?"

Finally Uncle Rolf turned to them. "Now, what can I do for you?"

Thorfinn explained why they had travelled to Orkney. His uncle twiddled his moustache. "Hmm, I'm glad you came. Nobody knows more about cooking fish than me."

"That's just what we thought, dear Uncle," said Thorfinn.

"No one can smoke a flounder like me, or stuff a pike like me, or souse a sparling, or stew a redfish. No one can sautée a sturgeon the way I do. And yet..." An annoyed look came over his face. "When I put one of these down in front of a Viking, you know

47

what they do?" He threw his hands to his chest and his eyes welled up. "They curse me, they accuse me of poisoning them. I'm SOOOOOO unappreciated!"

"HUH! You can't blame them," said Olaf. "You might as well attack them with a hammer as put fish down for their dinner. YUCK!"

"Shut up, you!" cried Velda, nudging Olaf with her axe. Uncle Rolf continued, shaking his head. "It's such a pity the Vikings hate fish. The sea that surrounds us is the best in the world for seafood." He sank into his seat with a great sigh.

"So, can you help me?" asked Thorfinn.

Rolf leapt to his feet again. "Can I?" He took Thorfinn by the shoulder. "Young man, I will show you EVERYTHING I know about cooking fish: how to broil a stickleback, how to bake a perch, how to pickle herring. I'll even show you how to steam an eel. By the time I've finished with YOU, my lad, you will know as much as I do." Rolf rubbed his hands together. "Let's get started!"

Thorfinn grinned and rolled up his sleeves, just as Harek, who wasn't looking where he was going, tripped over a mop and bucket and fell flat on his face:

"AAAAARGH!"

Then got his foot stuck in the bucket.

"HEEELP!"

Oswald tried to help him.

"HEEAVVE!" cried the old man, sounding like a camel with allergies as he strained to pull the bucket off Harek's leg.

They were interrupted by a muffled voice: "Hello? HELLO? Is anyone there?" It was Torsten, who'd managed to get lost inside a cupboard.

Thorfinn turned to Velda. "My dear friend, would you mind awfully rounding up the others and taking them back to the ship. I might be a while."

Velda looked at the chaos the crew were causing in the kitchens. Gertrude was still shrieking, Torsten had tumbled out of the cupboard and was sprawled across the floor, and Grimm was curled up in a basket beside a dog with big sad eyes, blubbing his head off.

Oswald finally managed to pull the bucket off Harek's foot, but the final yank sent the old man toppling backwards over a table...

"EEEEEEE!"

...only to land on top of Grut, who was hiding there gobbling a pie he'd pinched from the chefs.

Velda rolled her sleeves up and said to Thorfinn, "I don't know who's got the tougher job – you or me. RIGHT YOU BUNCH OF LOSERS – BACK TO THE SHIP!"

# CHAPTER 6

Thorfinn began by watching his uncle closely.
Rolf prepared the fish at his worktable and then
transferred it onto a hot griddle.

"Your hands are moving so fast," said Thorfinn.

"You'll get used to it, lad!" replied Rolf.

And he was right, because Thorfinn was quick to
learn. Rolf soon gave Thorfinn a nod. "Your turn!"

Beads of sweat appeared on Thorfinn's brow as
he copied what his uncle showed him, but he was
smiling. "What fun this is!"

Before long the boy began to improve. By the

following day he could match his uncle in everything, until at last the two of them were sautéeing side by side. Indeed, they were soon working in harmony, cooking dishes together.

"Chuck me the swordfish steak, my lad!" his uncle would cry.

"Why most certainly, old bean," Thorfinn would reply, lobbing the juicy morsel high over his shoulder for Uncle Rolf to catch in his hot pan. This soon drew an audience, as the other chefs crowded round to watch.

It was three days before Thorfinn and Rolf returned to the pier-side to find the crew, who had managed to avoid any further accidents under Velda's watchful eye.

"Thanks to my dear uncle I now know everything there is to know about cooking fish. I can chargrill a bream, roast a charr, pan-fry a turbot. I can even griddle a grayling. We're going to host a wonderful feast for the King."

**"HUZZAH!"** cried the crew.

"Can we go home now?" said Olaf. "I'm sick of hanging around this boat with these idiots."

"Uh, I do hate going home, it's so boring!" said Grimm.

Thorfinn stepped aboard the boat and coughed to clear his throat. "My dear crew, we're going *fishing!*"

"Huzzooo!" they cried, with a lot less enthusiasm.

Uncle Rolf helped them to restock the ship's stores, and then it was time to continue their journey.

"Come back and visit any time," said Uncle Rolf as the boat moved away.

"Thanks again, Uncle," said Thorfinn.

"Remember, the best fish can be found in the wild ocean far to the west."

"He's right," said Oswald. "Legend has it that the seas there are jumping with exotic creatures."

"Very well, then. That's where we'll go," said Thorfinn. He turned to Torsten. "To the west!"

Torsten's face took on the look of a badly stuffed goat. "West, oh, er, right. Er, which way is that again?"

"Towards the setting sun, my dear friend," said Thorfinn.

Torsten nodded enthusiastically. "RIGHHHT! Thanks. That's easy. For the first time I know exactly which way to go." He bowed and turned to take charge of the ship's rudder. "Towards the setting sun!"

# CHAPTER 7

They left the Orkney Islands behind and sailed west. The sky was covered with thick cloud and the sea began to roll.

Gertrude spent all day cooking, and then waved what looked like a large brown blob under the crew's noses. "Anyone like a piece of me lovely sticky ant cake?"

Even Grut turned his nose up at it. "Great Thor! It's so sticky you could slap it between some bricks and build a house with it."

Velda was at the stern, practising her kicking.

# "HI-YAA!"

"Oh, will you knock it off with that stupid dance routine," said Olaf.

Velda fumed. "This is no dance routine. I HATE dancing. Dancing's for wimps. This is called kick-boxing."

"Rubbish!"

"It is too! It's an ancient art, taught to me by an old and wise master."

"Oh yeah? Who?"

Velda bit her lip and her eyes shifted to Oswald, who was propped up on his cane nearby.

"Him??" Olaf thumbed at the old man. "Ha! He'd lose a fight with a squirrel." Olaf's booming laugh rang out across the waves.

"Only because I'm saving myself, young man," said Oswald, sounding a bit like a squirrel – one that was gnawing on an especially large nut.

"Yeah, just you wait," said Velda. "One day, you'll see Oswald leap into action, then you'll be laughing on the other side of your face."

"I can't wait," Olaf chuckled.

Meanwhile Torsten and Thorfinn stood on the prow gazing ahead at the horizon.

"Pardon me, Mr Ship-Sinker," said Thorfinn, "but how do you tell which way we're headed if you can't see the sun?"

"Ah, that's why I have this." Torsten pulled a glass stone out of his pocket. "It's a sun stone. You hold it up to the clouds and it tells you where the sun is.

Look, I'll show you." He
held the stone up.

Harek, the clumsy
warrior, was mending a
broken plank on the deck
nearby. His hammer suddenly flew
out of his hand. "Whoops! Butterfingers!" he cried.

The hammer thumped Torsten on the back of the
head. "OW!" The stone flew through the air and –

# SPLASH!

– fell into the water. "NOOOOO!"

"SORR-EEE!" cried Harek, while Torsten's fingers
grasped at thin air.

"It's no good. It's gone."

"Er, right, is that bad?" asked Harek, looking embarrassed.

"Without it I have no way of seeing which way is west. So, yes, it's bad."

But the crew soon had more problems on their hands, when Velda pointed out a darker, thundery bank of cloud rolling towards them. "Look, a storm is coming!"

Thorfinn stepped up on a water barrel and coughed. "Ahem. Excuse me everyone. I do hate to interrupt, but would you please be so good as to help batten down the hatches?"

They all got to work, rolling up the sail, drawing in the oars and closing the oar ports. The boat was ready to face the storm. Everyone hunkered down on deck, waiting.

# CHAPTER 8

The storm was ferocious. For hours, the wind howled, the rain battered down, the boat tossed from side to side. Lots of supplies crashed over the side of the boat. Everyone held on tight, until eventually the waves calmed and the rain stopped.

"Check everything, see if she's still in good shape," said Thorfinn, and the crew inspected the boat.

Soon Harek began to yell. "Thorfinn, quick! There's a leak. We're taking on water."

Thorfinn and a few others rushed over to see water spurting up between two of the wooden

planks that made up the hull. Thorfinn stroked his chin. "Hmm, that is something of a bind."

"A bind?" yelled Olaf. "It's a disaster, that's what it is. We could drown!"

"We can fix it. We just need tools," said Grut.

"We don't have any. They all got washed over the side," said Harek.

The crew started bickering, and shouting over one another.

"It's your fault, you fool!" said Olaf to Torsten.

"It's Harek's fault, he lost my sun stone," replied Torsten.

"Oh, we're all doomed, this is SOOOO depressing," said Grimm.

"And me so young!" shrieked Gertrude.

To shut everyone up, Velda let loose a sharp, terrifying yell that would shatter glass chandeliers, had there been any glass chandeliers on board. There was silence. She nodded at Thorfinn, who nodded back and then stood up on a barrel.

"All we need to do is shore up the hole," said Thorfinn.

"But we don't have anything to use!" said Grut.

"We must be able to think of something."

Thorfinn turned to Oswald, who rubbed his beard between two fingers.

"We usually use hemp and pine tar to seal any leaks on board," he said.

"That all got washed away along with the tools," said Harek.

"We're DOOMED I tell you!" cried Grimm as he slumped down on a bucket.

Thorfinn turned to Gertrude. "My dear Mistress Grotty, would you please go and fetch your sticky ant pie?"

Her face creased into a smile. "Why, Thorfinn, of courses I will." She toddled off to fetch her cake. She seemed to be under the impression that Thorfinn actually intended to eat it.

Then Thorfinn turned to Oswald. "My dear old friend, you know those very large white underpants you wear? I don't suppose you have a spare pair we could borrow?"

Oswald looked offended. "No one's going to use MY underpants to plug a hole in a sinking ship."

"Oh please," said Velda. "We don't have anything else big enough."

"Oh, very well," grumbled the old man.

"And finally," said Thorfinn, "we need something strong and elastic." He turned to Grut. "My dear Mr Goat-Gobbler, do you have anything suitable?"

Grut flushed. His eyes darted from side to side. "Er, no."

"Oh come on, I know your secret. Don't worry, I won't tell," Thorfinn whispered loudly.

Everyone looked at each other, puzzled, except Thorfinn, who smiled, and Grut, whose face went even redder.

Grut sighed and his shoulders slumped. "OK." He opened his tunic and hauled out an enormous corset. The others gasped as his massive flabby belly exploded out of his shirt.

"A corset, ha!" Olaf fell about laughing. "He looks like a whale!"

Oswald returned, flinging his spare underpants at Thorfinn. They were practically the size of a tablecloth. Harek picked them up between his thumb and forefinger. "EEEWW!"

"They're clean!" said Oswald.

Harek began to stuff the underpants in the hole. The water slowed to a trickle.

Gertrude returned with her cake. "There you go me dears. Have a mouthful of sticky ants."

"Thank you," said Thorfinn. She was horrified to see him hand it to Harek, who smeared it into the gap. The water almost stopped altogether.

"Now we just need to hammer it in a bit," said Harek. "Except we don't have a hammer."

"No problem," said Thorfinn. He turned to Velda.

"My dear old pal, would you be so good as to put your excellent kicking into practice?"

Velda rolled up her sleeves. "You betya. Watch this." She delivered a mighty kick against the hull.

# "HI-YAA!"

Then another, and another. It wasn't long before the underpants and the sticky ant pie had been squashed flat and the hole sealed for good.

"Excellent work," said Thorfinn. "Now we'll nail it all in place using my friend Grut's corset." He handed it to Harek, who stretched it out to its tightest point and bashed nails in with an axe handle to pin it to the hull.

"All we need to do now is bail out the water," said Grut. "Are there any buckets left on board?"

"Oh, I suppose we could always use this one I'm sitting on," sighed Grimm. "But what's the point?"

"Shut up and hand me the bucket," said Harek.

"Well done, everyone," said Thorfinn. "We're saved!"

"**HUZZAH!**" they all cried, except for Olaf, who for once had nothing to say.

They gazed out at the horizon, wondering if the waves would guide them to the famous fishing grounds in the far west ocean.

# CHAPTER 9

The following morning they woke to find the boat surrounded by sea fog.

"There's fear in the crew's faces," said Oswald.

"And no wonder," said Torsten. "There's only one thing Vikings hate more than fog."

"Line dancing!" said Grut.

"No," replied Torsten. "Krakens, of course." Krakens were legendary sea monsters. Not that anyone had ever seen one.

"But my dear friend, krakens are just a myth," said Thorfinn.

"Exactly, and fog is very, very real," said Torsten. "We could crash into rocks and get shipwrecked."

"So what do we do?" asked Velda.

"There's nothing we can do. Just sit tight and wait."

"Why don't we try fishing?" said Thorfinn. "After all, it's why we're here."

The crew agreed, if only because there was nothing better to do. Harek quickly rigged up some fishing rods, and the crew dangled them over the side.

Unfortunately this venture wasn't very successful. All Gertrude managed to catch was an old boot. Grimm caught a bit of wood. Grut caught some seaweed, which tasted disgusting. Torsten wrestled for hours with something on the end of his fishing rod, only to find when he hauled it aboard that it was just a tiny perch. Velda and Thorfinn were the only ones to land any proper fish. And by this time the crew was so hungry they decided to eat them all. Except, that is, for Olaf.

"I don't care how hungry I am, I'm not eating FISH!"

**✳ ✳ ✳**

Eventually the fog lifted, pulling back from the ship like a shroud.

"Fabulous," said Thorfinn. "Though we still have no idea where we are."

Their problem soon solved itself when the lookout called, "Land ahoy!" He pointed out hills on the horizon.

"Land! **HUZZAH!**" The crew started celebrating.

They neared the shore and sailed slowly along, looking for a sheltered bay.

"Look, there's a good spot!" cried Torsten, and they beached the longship in the surf.

The crew jumped into the water, except for Oswald, who demanded to be carried. Unfortunately Harek tripped while carrying the old man through the waves.

"Arrgh! I'm all wet now, you great oaf!" Oswald sounded like an attacking seagull. He hit Harek with his cane until he got back up. "I've got chilblains, you know. This isn't helping!"

"OW! Gerroff! You ungrateful old goat!" Harek dumped the old man on the sand.

"Where are we?" asked Thorfinn as they lined up on the beach, staring at the rocky, tree-covered hillside.

"Maybe it's the New World," said Velda.

"Maybe we all died and went to hell," said Grimm.

"Maybe we should go hunting and cook dinner," said Grut.

"Maybe they'll have new types of insects to eat," said Gertrude. "YUM!"

"Now, let's see," said Oswald, dusting himself down. "If we've reached the New World then as far as I know the natives will be wearing head-dresses and speaking a language none of us will understand."

Just then, a spear landed with a **WHACK!**
at Thorfinn's feet.

"Oh dear."

# CHAPTER 10

Dozens of armed warriors appeared from behind rocks and trees, aiming their weapons right at Thorfinn and his crew.

"Well, they're not wearing head-dresses," said Velda. In fact, they were wearing tartan.

"Kilts – well that's odd!" said Oswald.

One of the men stepped forward, large and hairy and snarling. "FREEZE! YA BUNCH O' EEJITS!"

"Hmm, I'm not sure I understand the language," said Thorfinn. He stepped forward and raised his palms towards the men. "My dear inhabitants of the

New World, we come in peace!"

Then Thorfinn started behaving very strangely. He began miming, acting out their voyage. He went from hauling anchor, to gazing from the prow of the ship, to getting caught in the storm.

"What by Odin's beard are you doing?" cried Olaf. "Vikings don't play charades."

"They're bound to understand sign language, old friend."

The warriors' snarly leader waved his sword at him. "Whit's that daft gowk up tae?"

"Just a minute," said Velda. "I've heard that language before. It sounds like Scottish."

"Do they talk Scottish in the New World?" asked Harek.

"I wonder if they have any haggis on them. I'm starving!" said Grut.

"Ask them if they have any wee beasties for my cooking pot," said Gertrude.

"Why bother? Look at those swords. We're all

going to die!" moaned Grimm.

"Don't be ridiculous!" said Olaf. "Don't you get it? We haven't landed in the New World at all. We've landed in Scotland."

"AHHHH!" they all said at once.

"That does explain things, I suppose." Thorfinn turned to the snarly man. "Please don't shoot!"

The man raised his hand and his men lowered their weapons.

"It's alright, they're just Vikings," he said.

Olaf fumed. "What do you mean, JUST Vikings? You should be terrified."

"Aye, maybe. But you're no' whit we're most scared of, and you're no' the reason why we're here," replied the man. "We saw your boat's dragon head, that's all. We thought for a minute you were another sea monster come tae attack us."

"Wait – what do you mean, ANOTHER sea monster?" asked Velda.

"Aye, another." The man looked scared. "My name is Dougal, and we are the MacDonalds of Morar. You'd better come wi' us." He led them off the beach, up the cliff and through the trees until they came to a small fishing village. One side of the village faced the sea and the other faced a beautiful loch fringed by mountains. "This is where we live. We can fish in salt water and in fresh water."

"How ingenious!" said Oswald.

"Scenery! How tiresome," said Grimm.

"How about that haggis?" asked Grut, his stomach rumbling loudly.

"Can someone remind me where my boat is parked?" said Torsten.

"AAAARGH!" cried Harek as he tripped and fell down a well.

"Midgies!" yelped Gertrude, jumping up and down with glee. "Oh, we'll haves us midgie pie tonight."

Dougal led them into the village hall, where the clan had gathered for a meeting. All eyes fearfully turned to the newcomers.

Dougal slumped down on the chieftain's chair. His snarl disappeared. "Ye've come at a bad time. There's a ferocious dragon in the loch. It keeps attacking our fishing boats."

"What a strange fix," said Thorfinn.

"We'd give anything to be rid us o' this creature." said Dougal.

"Ha!" laughed Olaf. "I don't know what it has to do with us."

"We're looking for fish," said Thorfinn.

"We have loads," said Dougal. "We've got some of the best and most interesting seafood in the whole celtic world."

"How fascinating!" said Thorfinn.

"We'll give you all you can carry if ye'll help us."

"What a kind offer," said Thorfinn. He looked round at his crew's faces. "Well, what do you say?"

They looked like they'd just been asked to jump off a tall cliff.

Except for Velda, who rolled up her sleeves.

"We're Vikings. We eat sea monsters for breakfast!"

# CHAPTER 11

Dawn the next morning found the entire crew crammed into a tiny fishing boat in the middle of the loch. They stared out in fear at the misty water. Harek wielded a giant fishing rod with a large chunk of fish as bait.

"I can think of better ways to spend a morning," said Olaf, squashed in beside Grimm. "For example, NOT trying to attract the attention of a massive sea monster."

"But if we succeed," said Thorfinn, "think of all the fish we'll take home with us."

The water was still, without even a ripple, for
hours and hours. Then there was a false alarm
when the boat shook violently from side to side.

"WHAT!? What's that?" cried Grut.

"Relax, it's just Oswald scratching his bottom,"
said Velda.

"I can't help it!" cried Oswald. "I've been wearing the same underpants for a week!"

Another hour passed. The sun rose higher and it became quite hot. "There isn't really a monster," yawned Torsten. "Sea monsters are a myth."

"Maybe it's all a trick and they've left us out here to die," said Grimm.

"Maybe they were just imagining things..." Oswald was saying, when suddenly from behind there came a colossal...

# WHOOOOSH!

Showers of water poured over them. A giant shadow blotted out the sun. Out of the water rose a solid wall of slimy green scales. They looked up...

...and up...

...and up!

A long slender neck ended in a reptilian head, and a pair of yellow snake eyes glared down at them.

Harek's hand was left holding thin air, as the fishing rod was now sticking out of the creature's mouth. The monster crunched on it then spat it out.

Harek slowly rose and drew his sword. "Nobody move. Leave this to me-EEEE!" He slipped and tumbled loudly into the water. **SPLOSH!**

"We're definitely doomed now," moaned Grimm.

Grut's stomach grumbled. "Imagine eating that thing!"

Gertrude whipped out her cooking pot and started bashing it with her spoon. "Hee hee hee!" she cackled. "Into my pot wee beastie!"

Olaf's face was white. "Right, stuff you lot, I'm off!" He dived into the water and swam for the shore.

Velda leaned back and let loose an enormous kick in midair. "HI-YAA monster! Don't mess with me!"

Oswald stroked his beard with one hand and scratched his bum with the other. "Fascinating!"

All eyes turned to Thorfinn, who rose to his feet then did something very strange. Something no human had ever done to this creature before.

He smiled.

"Good day to you, my dear friend. What a beautiful afternoon!"

Some time later, one of the village boys burst into the hall, where Dougal was holding a meeting. "Chief, ye've got tae come an' see this!"

Dougal and his men scrambled for their weapons and rushed outside to find the strangest sight they had ever set eyes on.

The giant sea monster that had been terrorising their village for so long was propped up on the lochside basking in the sun, surrounded by Thorfinn, his crew, and the rest of the villagers. Instead of attacking it with spears and swords, the villagers were stroking it. Children were climbing on its back. Thorfinn was feeding the creature fish from his hand, and his pet pigeon Percy was perched on its head.

"Come closer everyone," Thorfinn was saying. "Don't be scared. She loves children."

Dougal pushed his way through the crowd. "Whit's going on?"

"Her name is Morag," said Thorfinn. "She's been attacking your boats because she's hungry. You've been taking too many fish from the loch, leaving her with nothing to eat. But it's OK, we've reached an agreement. You just need to share, and you'll be the best of friends."

# CHAPTER 12

Thorfinn and his crew set off once again, their longship packed full of fish, caught from the sea, not from Morag's loch, and packed in salt for the journey.

"Fareweel and thanks for everything!" cried Dougal from the beach as the ship sailed away.

Velda turned to Thorfinn. "Mission accomplished! Now we just have to get back home in time for the feast."

"By my calculations we have just four days," said Oswald.

"No problem," Thorfinn replied. He turned to Torsten.

"My dear Mr Ship-Sinker, would you please head north."
Torsten looked confused. "Or rather, up the way."

Torsten smiled. "That's what I like about you,
Thorfinn: you talk my language."

# ❊ ❊ ❊

After exactly four days of rolling seas they finally
spotted the Norwegian coast.

"Ahoy! There's home," cried Velda, the lookout, pointing
at the mountainous entrance to their own fjord.

"**HUZZAH!**" cried the crew. "THREE CHEERS
FOR THORFINN!" If Oswald was right, they should
make it just in time for the King's arrival.

Everyone was celebrating, except for Grimm. "Not
here again!" he grumbled.

And Olaf. "I can't believe it! How did I manage to survive a voyage with this mob!"

Most of the village turned out to greet them at the pier. Thorfinn's father, Harald, swung his son into the air. "Well done, my boy! You're just in time. The King and his party are on their way."

"In that case, dear friends," said Thorfinn, turning to his crew, "would you please unload the fish and take them up to the kitchens?"

Just then, a horn sounded. All eyes turned to the King's procession, which was snaking around the edge of the fjord towards them. The villagers lined the streets, and Thorfinn and Velda had to climb a wall to get a decent view.

The procession was led by knights, and squires

carrying banners. A troop of ferocious Viking warriors followed – the King's personal bodyguards. Then came the rich nobles, and finally the King and Queen, bedecked in jewels, wearing gold and crimson robes.

Everyone bowed. Harald spotted Magnus the Bone-Breaker, the chief of the next village, who had followed the procession. He had an especially smug grin on his face as he waved at them.

Harald turned to Thorfinn. "I'll welcome the King and Queen. You'd better get cooking."

Thorfinn and Velda ran to the kitchens, but found Olaf's father, Erik the Ear-Masher, waiting outside.

"We asked around for volunteers to help you with the feast," he said.

"Oh, goodie!" said Thorfinn.

"Here they are." He swung open the door to reveal Thorfinn's crew. All of them. They were dressed in white aprons and wearing chef's hats. Even Olaf was there, shaking his head. "Great Thor, why did I agree to this?"

# CHAPTER 13

The kitchen was filled with hustle and bustle.
Thorfinn showed the others how to clean and cut
the fish but he did most of the cooking himself.

"Can I not puts ANY insects in?" howled
Gertrude.

"I'm afraid we can't, old friend," said Thorfinn.

"Awwww!" She made a sign with her forefinger
and thumb. "Just a LEETLE bit?"

"Oh, can't we eat some? I'm starving!" said Grut,
licking his lips.

"NO!" said Velda. "It's for the King and Queen."

Grimm spent most of the time gazing into the glassy eyes of a giant haddock. "Oh, this poor fish!"

As for Torsten, he went outside to find more wood for the fire, but he never came back...

Harek grabbed a meat cleaver and grinned. "What can I do to help?"

Everyone eyed him fearfully.

"Er, tell you what," said Velda, carefully prising the cleaver out of his hands. "Why don't you go and look for Torsten?"

"Right you are!" he replied, and left. The others sighed with relief.

At one point Magnus the Bone-Breaker wandered into the kitchen. He was being nosy and looking over everyone's shoulders.

"What do *you* want?" asked Velda.

"Oh, charming!" he replied. "I only came in to congratulate you on the success of your voyage."

Velda waved a cod threateningly in his direction. "Well, buzz off! We're busy."

"OK, OK!" Magnus shrank back, but he lingered for a while, gawping at all the fish and prodding them in disgust.

After hours of hard work, the large table in the middle of the kitchen was stacked with huge platters of food. Dozens of different types of fish had been cooked in dozens of different ways.

Velda wiped the back of her hand across her brow. "Phew!"

Harald burst in from the door that led to the great hall, accompanied by the raucous sound of laughter. The King and his party were ready for their feast.

"Well?" said Harald.

"Yes, Father, it's all ready," said Thorfinn.

"Good!" A line of stewards filed in. Harald nodded at them. They picked up the platters one by one and hoisted them onto their shoulders. "Here we go!"

Harald and Thorfinn led the stewards into the great hall where the King and Queen were sitting on thrones behind a long table, bedecked in robes and jewels. Knights and attendants stood to attention at their sides.

Harald bowed before them. He looked about as comfortable as a caveman at a posh tea party. "Your Majesties, I hope you enjoy our humble feast."

The King arose and looked down his nose at Thorfinn. "This... boy... is your head chef?"

"Yes, Sire," replied Harald. "He's the best chef in our village. I'm sure you'll find the food to your liking."

Magnus the Bone-Breaker, who was standing at the King's side, guffawed. "A boy indeed!"

The Queen arose from her seat, smiling and looking radiant. She touched her husband's arm. "My dear, I think it will be wonderful. Tell me, is that seafood? I absolutely LOVE seafood."

Thorfinn grinned. "Why, yes, your Majesty, it is."

The King gave a slight groan. "Ugh, seafood, must we? It's not a very Viking thing to eat, is it?"

"It certainly is not," chipped in Magnus. "This village is rubbish!"

Thorfinn gestured at the giant platters being laid before the royal couple. "I assure you, this is the best seafood in the world, and it's all responsibly sourced. No sea monsters were harmed. Perhaps you might like to try the devilled whitebait, the sozzled lampreys, the jellied eels..."

The King yawned. "Oh, very well."

The Queen clapped her hands together. "How exciting. So many lovely fish to try. Why don't you go first, dear?"

The King nodded and picked up a slice of smoked salmon. He eyed it warily. All the other Vikings in the room screwed up their faces in disgust.

"The things I do for my wife." He was about to pop the salmon into his mouth when the sound of groaning filled the hall.

# CHAPTER 14

"Ohhhh! Ow! Ow! Ow! Ow!"

"What's that?" said Harald.

The King paused. The groaning was coming from behind one of the tables. Erik pulled the table away to find Grut writhing around on the floor holding his stomach.

"What's wrong with you?" demanded Erik.

"Ow! Sorry, I pinched some food," he said. "Ow! Ow! Ow! I think it's the salmon."

Velda leapt forward onto the table, swinging from the rafters. She landed on her feet in front of the King.

"STOP THE FEAST! Something is wrong with the food," she shouted.

"Hmm, I'm afraid she may be right," said Thorfinn.

"WHAT?!" Harald flung his hands to his head. "How could this happen?"

Erik's face crumpled. "What a disaster!"

Oswald knelt down to examine Grut. After a moment he rose to his feet. "I'm afraid it's poison.

Someone has poisoned the food." He sounded like an aardvark with a blocked nose.

"POISON!" Everyone in the room gasped. Harald's face was ashen. The King and Queen were shocked.

"Oh dear!" said Thorfinn. "Will Mr Goat-Gobbler be alright?"

"I'm not sure yet. It depends what type of poison it is." Oswald began sniffing the platters, in particular the platter of smoked salmon that the King was about to eat from. "Hmmm."

"This is an outrage!" cried Magnus, looking dramatically outraged. He leaned in to the King. "Your Majesty, someone here has tried to poison you. The entire village should be burned to the ground."

"No," replied the King. "If someone has poisoned

the food then whoever is in charge of the food is to blame." He turned to his guards. "Arrest the chef."

"Dear me, I wouldn't dream of such a thing," Thorfinn laughed. Two guards grabbed Thorfinn's arm.

"No, wait!" cried Harald, heading for the guards.

Magnus blocked his way. "Yes, quite right," he addressed the King. "But you should burn the village down anyway; it spoils the view for all the tourists."

"Oh not again," the Queen protested. "It so saddens me to see you burning villages."

The King hesitated for a moment, then looked to his wife. "Very well, dear, as you wish. But take the chef to the stocks!"

"Yes," said Magnus, "and pelt him with rotten fruit."

Gertrude jumped in front of the King and flung

her arms out. "No, nots Thorfinn. Why would Thorfinn poison the King? Why?"

"Who cares?" said Magnus. "He's the one in charge, so it's his fault. Are you questioning his Majesty?" He turned again to the King. "You see how insubordinate this lot are. How about catapulting them all into the sea, instead? I've got a cartload of tourists who'd pay to watch."

Oswald was still sniffing the platters on the table. He raised his head. "Thorfinn had no reason to poison the King and bring disaster to our village. We need to find out who poisoned the food."

But the guards weren't listening. They were dragging Thorfinn towards the door.

# CHAPTER 15

"You can't do this to Thorfinn!" cried Velda, jumping between him and the door, her arms outstretched, while Percy flapped at the men's heads to try and put them off. The room fell silent.

"It's quite alright," said Oswald. "You can continue with the feast. Only the smoked salmon was poisoned."

"But how do you know?" asked Harald.

"I know what poison was used – the juice from an arctic berry that grows in the hills above the fjord. It has a zingy, acidy smell, which I can only smell on this one platter."

"Are you sure?" Harald picked up a fork and sampled one of the other platters. After a moment, he shrugged. "Tastes about as fine as fish tastes, which is pretty yucky."

"Pardon me, old friend," said Thorfinn, who wasn't remotely bothered that two burly guards were manhandling him. "But what about poor Mr Goat-Gobbler? Is the poison dangerous?"

Oswald shook his head. "The berries are only mildly poisonous to humans, just enough to give the King and Queen a stomach upset. But it would have been more than enough reason for the King to burn down our village." Oswald turned and fixed his brow on Magnus. "And who do we know that wants rid of our village?"

Meanwhile, Percy landed on Magnus's shoulder and started nibbling at a small pouch that was hanging from his breast strap.

"Why are you looking at me?" asked Magnus.

"Hey, he was in the kitchen snooping around while we were cooking," said Velda. "I wondered what he was up to."

"Those berries may be poisonous to humans, but birds love them," said Oswald.

Suddenly the pouch burst open and hundreds of tiny red berries spewed out. Magnus glanced down at the mound on the floor, then looked up. Everyone in the room, including the King, was glaring at him.

"Of course you did it!" said Harald, his eye twitching fiercely. "You wanted our village burnt down to make way for your four-wheel-drive chariot tours."

Magnus began retreating. "Now look, it's nothing personal, business is business."

He backed into Gertrude, who whacked him on the head with a frying pan.

BOIIIIIINNNNNGGGG!

"OW! That REALLY hurt!" He rubbed his head, dodged round her and ran towards the kitchen.

"STOP HIM!" cried Harald.

Grut stepped in the way and thrust out his belly. Magnus bounced off it.

# BOIIIIIINNNNNGGGG!

He reeled in front of Velda, who yelled and thrust her leg at his face.

# "HI-YAA!"

He parried the kick away. "You'll have to do better than that, little girl." Magnus turned to find Oswald staring at him from close range. "What's this, old man?"

Oswald suddenly dropped his stick and jumped

in the air. His legs cracked
apart and his heel
SMACKED against
Magnus's chin.

"HI-YAA!"

He sounded like an
albatross throwing up.

"OOF!" Magnus's eyes crossed
for a moment and he staggered.

Velda turned to Olaf. "See? I told you he's an
old master."

"And I told you I was saving myself," added Oswald.

Olaf puffed out his cheeks. "Well, you learn
something new every day!"

Magnus looked around frantically for another escape route, then dived out the window...

# CRASH

...into the chicken coop outside. There was a barrage of angry clucking from the chickens.

Thorfinn threw open the door of the great hall to see him tearing away, chased by a dozen pecking birds.

Up ahead, Harek was crossing the street carrying a very long plank of wood. He was on his way to repair the hull of their longship. Magnus ducked underneath the plank and kept running.

Velda put her fingers in her mouth and whistled. "Hey, Harek!"

Harek turned round, and so did the long wooden plank.

# WHACK!

Magnus crashed to the ground, while Harek waved back at Velda. "COO-EEE!"

Thorfinn turned to his father and beamed proudly. "They're a great team, my crew, aren't they?"

# CHAPTER 16

Magnus was dragged away by the guards, while the Queen tried the food and assured everyone it was delicious.

"How lovely," said Thorfinn. "Now, if I may, I'd best make a start on the washing-up." He bowed, then returned to the kitchens with Percy, leaving everyone else to enjoy the feast.

A short while later his crew burst in to find him and Percy at the sink. Thorfinn's sleeves were rolled up, and he was calmly scrubbing pots and humming to himself.

"Thorfinn, the feast was a great success!" cried Velda. "The Queen said the pickled sturgeon was the best she had ever tasted."

"And the seared plaice... and the stuffed turbot... and the charbroiled bream!" added an even-more-excited-if-that's-even-possible Harek.

Harald was with them too. "This will be the making of our village."

A cry soon went up through the hall: "BRING IN THE CHEF!"

"The Queen wants to thank you,'" said Harald.

Gertrude nudged Thorfinn. "On you goes boss! You've earned it."

"My dear friends," replied Thorfinn with a little smile. "We all did this together. Either we go in as a team or not at all."

So, a moment later Thorfinn entered the great hall leading his entire crew, all dressed up in their white chefs' outfits. Even Grut, who was still suffering and had to be carried in by Torsten and Harek.

Everyone – including the King and Queen – stood and cheered. "That was the best seafood I have ever tasted, Thorfinn," the Queen said. "And this has truly been our finest feast."

"Well done, young man," added the King. "And thanks to your pet for identifying the true poisoner."

Percy seemed to bow from his perch on Thorfinn's shoulder.

"Did I mention he's my son, your Highness?" replied Harald.

"Indeed? Then you should be very proud."

Harald beamed. "I am."

"Pleeeaase come back again, your Highnesses," screeched Gertrude. "Next time I'll cooks you a nice dung-beetle hotpot."

At that point the applause stopped.

After the feast, Harald, Erik and the others dragged Magnus to the marketplace where they locked him in the stocks and pelted him with fruit and vegetables.

"You can't do this!" Magnus yelled. "I'm a chief! It's not fair!"

"Think yourself lucky, Bone-Breaker!" cried Erik. "If it wasn't for the Queen begging for your life you'd have been catapulted into the sea."

"I beg your pardon, dear Father," said Thorfinn, interrupting Harald just as he was launching a giant soggy cauliflower towards Magnus's head. "I do so hate to bother you, but what shall I do with all the leftover fish?"

Harald's eyes lit up. "I have a great idea." He divided out the remaining fish between Thorfinn's crew. "Let's chuck them at Magnus."

"OUCH! YUCK! STOP IT!" Magnus cried as they bombarded him. "I HATE fish!"

"So do we!" cried Velda as she span round like a discus thrower and let loose a giant flounder towards his face.

"It's DIS-*GUSTING!*" cried Gertrude.

"Oh dear." Thorfinn shook his head. "What a strange and delightful bunch." He tapped his shoulder and Percy flapped onto it. "There's a good bird. Now let's go home for tea."

RICHARD THE PICTURE-CONQUEROR

DAVID THE STORY-CHIEF

**DAVID MACPHAIL** left home at eighteen to travel the world and have adventures. After working as a chicken wrangler, a ghost-tour guide and a waiter on a tropical island, he now has the sensible job of writing about yetis and Vikings. At home in Perthshire, Scotland, he exists on a diet of cream buns and zombie movies.

**RICHARD MORGAN** was born and raised by goblins on the Yorkshire moors. After running away to New Zealand to play with yachts and paint backgrounds for Disney TV he returned to the UK to write and illustrate children's books. He now lives in Cambridge, England, and has a family of goblins of his own.

# WHICH VIKING ARE YOU?

Pick *one* of the four answers for each question to find out which Viking character you are most like.

**1. You're redecorating your room. What colour do you go for?**
A) Mud.
B) Blood red.
C) Ooh! Purple, mauve or orchid please.
D) Sounds like too much hard work. I'm off for a snooze.

**2. What's your favourite type of scone?**
A) Scones?! PAH! Yuck!
B) Overcooked, hard ones that I can catapult at the enemy!
C) All flavours are equally delightful!
D) I don't mind, so long as there's jam.

**3. How do you like to spend your weekends?**
A) Exactly the same as my weekdays – raiding, burning and burping!
B) Practising my axe throwing.
C) Perhaps some home baking, a spot of DIY, followed by a nice cup of tea.
D) I'll take some tea and snacks, thanks, and a nice lie down.

## 4. Which animal would you choose as a pet?

A) A ferocious sea monster.

B) I'll tame a wild wolf!

C) A friendly pigeon.

D) Something obedient – a goldfish perhaps.

## 5. The man sitting next to you is eating FISH. What do you do?

A) By Odin, no one eats fish near me! I'd challenge him to a sword fight.

B) Not more fish?! I'd stab it with my dagger and fling it away.

C) How delicious! I do enjoy seafood.

D) Ooh, does that mean I'm sitting down too? Lovely. I'd have a quick snooze.

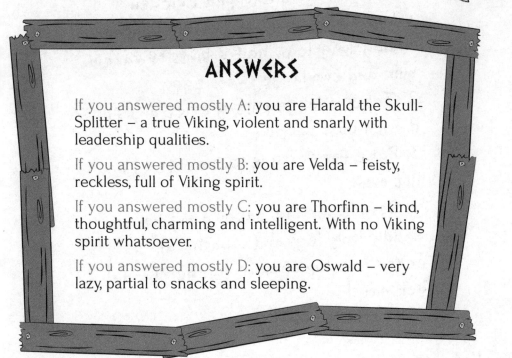

# ANSWERS

If you answered mostly A: you are Harald the Skull-Splitter – a true Viking, violent and snarly with leadership qualities.

If you answered mostly B: you are Velda – feisty, reckless, full of Viking spirit.

If you answered mostly C: you are Thorfinn – kind, thoughtful, charming and intelligent. With no Viking spirit whatsoever.

If you answered mostly D: you are Oswald – very lazy, partial to snacks and sleeping.

# GERTRUDE'S RECIPE CORNER

Your foods is DISGUSTING, so I has decided to gives you some help. Here is some of my favourite recipes.

## CHICKEN AND DADDY-LONG-LEGS QUICHE

1. Mixes up some chopped chicken with half a pounds of freshly squished daddy-long-legs, half a pints of rancid milk and two large swans eggs.

2. Takes a large pastry crust and fill it with your mixture.

3. Bake for forty leetle minuteses in a hot oven.

4. Before serving, takes a big deads daddy-long-legs and squash at across the top of your quiche. Ta-da! Delishious!

# SHEEP'S HEAD AND WOODLICE BROTH

1. Takes a large sheep's head and fry in a big pan with onions.
2. Once the head is brown and crusty adds 2 pints of elk stock.
3. Then adds in half a pounds of woodlice to gives your dish a nice woody flavour and chewy texture.
4. Leaves to simmer for an hour, then takes some sheep's eyeballs, with the stringy bits attached, and adds to your broth.
5. Serves steaming hot in bowls, with blindfolds. Some strange peoples don't like their foods staring at them.

P.S. Please remembers, I is proud to be an insectarian. I only uses insects that has already dropped deads.

## GERTRUDE

# VIKING RIDDLES!

**1.** There are seven Viking children standing in a row. Half of them are girls. How can this be?

**2.** What is lighter than one of Percy's feathers, but even Harald the Skull-Splitter would struggle to hold it?

**3.** What gets wetter and smellier the more it dries?

**4.** Which weighs more: a tonne of goldfish or a tonne of hungry sea monsters?

1. They're ALL girls. The boys are too busy fighting. **2.** His breath. **3.** A bearskin towel. **4.** They both weigh a tonne, you nitwits.

PERCY THE PIGEON HAS BROUGHT
THORFINN A SECRET MESSAGE.
CAN YOU DECODE IT TO WARN HIM?

CHECK   LE   P3LLL3N.   THESE'S   4

\_ \_ \_ \_ \_   \_ \_   \_ \_ \_ \_ \_ \_ \_ .   \_ \_ \_ \_ \_ \_   \_

PONGY   PLOT   4F33T   T3   P3LLL3N

\_ \_ \_ \_ \_   \_ \_ \_ \_   \_ \_ \_ \_ \_   \_ \_   \_ \_ \_ \_ \_ \_

THE   KING   3R   N38W4Y   4T

\_ \_ \_   \_ \_ \_ \_   \_ \_   \_ \_ \_ \_ \_ \_   \_ \_

Y3U8   DISGUSTING   R641T!

\_ \_ \_ \_   \_ \_ \_ \_ \_ \_ \_ \_ \_ \_   \_ \_ \_ \_ \_ !

| A | B | C | D | E | F | G | H | I | J | K | L | M |
|---|---|---|---|---|---|---|---|---|---|---|---|---|
| (rune) | (rune) | (rune) | (rune) | (rune) | (rune) | (rune) | (rune) | (rune) | (rune) | (rune) | (rune) | (rune) |

| N | O | P | Q | R | S | T | U | V | W | X | Y | Z |
|---|---|---|---|---|---|---|---|---|---|---|---|---|
| (rune) | (rune) | (rune) | (rune) | (rune) | (rune) | (rune) | (rune) | (rune) | (rune) | (rune) | (rune) | (rune) |

# PERCY THE PIGEON POST

EST. 799AD    ODINSDAY 18TH FEBRUARY    PRICE: ONE FRONT TOOTH

## SKULL-SPLITTING NEWS

In what will forever be known as the **Awful Invasion** the Scots have narrowly missed being invaded by a band of maurauding Vikings, led by the fearsome Chief of Indgar, Harald the Skull-Splitter.

## SPORTING HEADLINES

It is the weekend of the annual **Gruesome Games**. Word on the beach is that Thorfinn and his motley team have to save their village from the clutches of Magnus the Bone-Breaker. Odds are on for a new Chief of Indgar by Monday.

## FOULSOME FOOD

It's all about Le Poisson (that's FISH to you boneheads). The King of Norway is on his way to Indgar and he expects a most **Disgusting Feast**. But there's a poisoner at large and the heat is on in the kitchen...

## TORTUROUS TRAVEL

Early booking is essential to visit the **Rotten Scots'** most famous prisoner (that's Thorfinn) at Castle Red Wolf. Hurry — he may be rescued at any moment!

## LOST AND NOT FOUND

A massive hoard of **Terrible Treasure** stolen from the pesky Scots has mysteriously vanished. Large reward promised for information leading to its recovery.

## MISSING PERSONS

The **Raging Raiders** are prime suspects in the kidnapping of one harassed, goat-carrying Viking mum. Please report any sightings to Chief Harald the Skull-Splitter.

*Collect all of Thorfinn's adventures*